mo

p

library

montclair new jersey

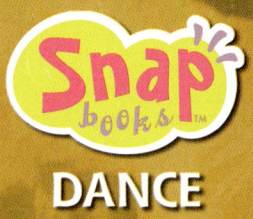

DANCE

Jazz Dance

by Wendy Garofoli

Consultant:
Jon Lehrer, Founder/Director of LehrerDance
Former Associate Director of Giordano Jazz Dance Chicago

Capstone press

Mankato, Minnesota

Snap Books are published by Capstone Press,
151 Good Counsel Drive, P.O. Box 669, Mankato, Minnesota 56002.
www.capstonepress.com

Copyright © 2008 by Capstone Press, a Capstone Publishers company.
All rights reserved. No part of this publication may be reproduced in whole
or in part, or stored in a retrieval system, or transmitted in any form or by
any means, electronic, mechanical, photocopying, recording, or otherwise,
without written permission of the publisher.
For information regarding permission, write to Capstone Press,
151 Good Counsel Drive, P.O. Box 669, Dept. R, Mankato, Minnesota 56002.
Printed in the United States of America

Library of Congress Cataloging-in-Publication Data
Garofoli, Wendy.
   Jazz dance / by Wendy Garofoli.
   p. cm. — (Snap books. Dance)
   Summary: "Describes jazz dance, including history and basic
steps" — Provided by publisher.
   Includes bibliographical references and index.
   ISBN-13: 978-1-4296-1352-1 (hardcover)
   ISBN-10: 1-4296-1352-1 (hardcover)
   1. Jazz dance. I. Title. II. Series.
GV1784.G37 2008
793.3 — dc22   2007023627

Editor: Jennifer Besel

Designer: Veronica Bianchini

Photo Researcher: Jo Miller

Photo Credits:

Capstone Press/Karon Dubke, cover, 2, 8–9, 10 (all), 11, 12 (all), 13, 14 (all), 15, 16 (all), 17 (all), 18, 19, 22, 23,
    24 (all), 25, 29
Corbis/Robbie Jack, 5; Rueters/Mark Wallheiser, 20
Courtesy of the author Wendy Garofoli, 32
Getty Images Inc./Evan Agostini, 21; Time Life Pictures/Gjon Mili, 6; Time Life Pictures/Ray Fisher, 7
ZUMA Press/The Tribune/Josh Birnbaum, 26–27

Acknowledgements:
Capstone Press thanks Mitzi Roberts and Dance Express in Mankato, Minnesota, for their assistance
preparing this book.

1 2 3 4 5 6 13 12 11 10 09 08

Table of Contents

Chapter 1
Jazz Dance: Then and Now 4

Chapter 2
Melting Pot of Dance 8

Chapter 3
Movin' to Your Own Beat 14

Chapter 4
Beyond Classic 18

Chapter 5
Takin' It to the Next Step 26

Glossary 30

Fast Facts 30

Read More 31

Internet Sites 31

About the Author 32

Index 32

CHAPTER ONE

Jazz Dance: Then and Now

Ever dream of performing in a show-stopping musical on Broadway? Or leaping across the stage at a dance competition? Or kicking up your heels with a dance company? Each of these activities is different. But they do have one thing in common — they use jazz dance.

What is jazz dance? It started out as a style of dance performed to jazz music in the 1920s. But jazz dance has changed over time. Today, it uses moves from modern, ballet, African, Caribbean, Latin, and even East Indian dance. Jazz will take you in many directions. And all those directions are full of energy, excitement, and tons of fun!

EARLY JAZZ

In the 1920s, jazz was the most popular music in the United States. People gathered and danced to this lively music in nightclubs. But unlike ballroom or ballet, the new jazz style was done with the knees and upper body bent. This body movement allowed people to dance fast, loose, and natural. And it also led to one of the key elements of jazz — individual style.

In the 1930s, dancers took jazz to another level. They performed dances like the Lindy hop to the fun big band music of the time. This kind of jazz was a more energetic, fast-paced dance. But that wasn't the end of jazz's show-stopping ways.

Jazz Master

Jack Cole is called the father of jazz dance. His style and technique have been studied and copied for years. A Broadway and Hollywood choreographer, Cole started as a modern dancer. He used his technical training to create his own style in the 1940s. Many of his dances used Hindu, Spanish, and ballet dances mixed with jazz moves. He paved the way for modern jazz choreographers. Many of today's jazz steps come from Cole and his followers.

CHAPTER TWO

Melting Pot of Dance

Today, jazz is a melting pot of popular styles. It changes with the times, just like popular music. Jazz dance allows dancers to express themselves. Today, jazz dance can be used with pop, rhythm and blues, rock, and many other sounds. Because of the variety, there are many styles of jazz dance. There's classic jazz, like the styles performed by Jack Cole and Gus Giordano. There's contemporary, which combines modern and jazz. There's even a style called jazz/funk, which borrows moves from hip-hop.

Class Act

Most U.S. dance studios offer jazz as a class. As a beginner, you'll likely start with classic jazz style before branching out into the more advanced styles. Learning classic jazz will provide a good foundation for becoming a well-rounded jazz dancer.

WHAT TO WEAR

Dance studios often have a dress code for jazz class. Before you sign up, call and ask what attire they require. You usually can't go wrong with a black leotard and tight black jazz pants.

You'll need specific shoes for each style of jazz. In classic jazz, you'll wear lace-up or slip-on jazz shoes. In more advanced classes, you'll need character shoes with heels and a buckle across the ankle. In contemporary or lyrical classes, you might only wear a protective covering on the balls of your bare feet. And in jazz/funk you can wear jazz sneakers.

WARMING UP

A jazz warm-up is all about getting loosened up. Roll your shoulders to warm up your upper body. Try moving your rib cage side to side and stretching to the side with your arms overhead. It's important to stretch your midsection and back because those muscles are used often in jazz.

To warm up your legs, lie on your back and pull each knee into your chest, one at a time. Keep your other leg straight on the ground as you hold your opposite knee.

Get your heart rate going by doing some jazz runs across the floor. Run with your knees bent. Try to stay low to the ground and take big steps. You should feel like you are coasting across the floor.

CHAPTER THREE

Movin' to Your Own Beat

A big part of jazz dance is moving to your own beat. Classic jazz maintains a lot of the moves from early jazz. Your knees are relaxed and your torso is loose. Also, syncopated rhythms, like the ones used in jazz music, are important aspects of classic jazz. Not every move follows a steady beat. Instead, some steps are long, while others are quick and sharp.

Another key element of classic jazz is body isolation. When you isolate a certain part of the body, you separate it from other parts. Imagine keeping your shoulders straight as you move your head side to side. Isolations aren't super easy to do, but they are awesome to see.

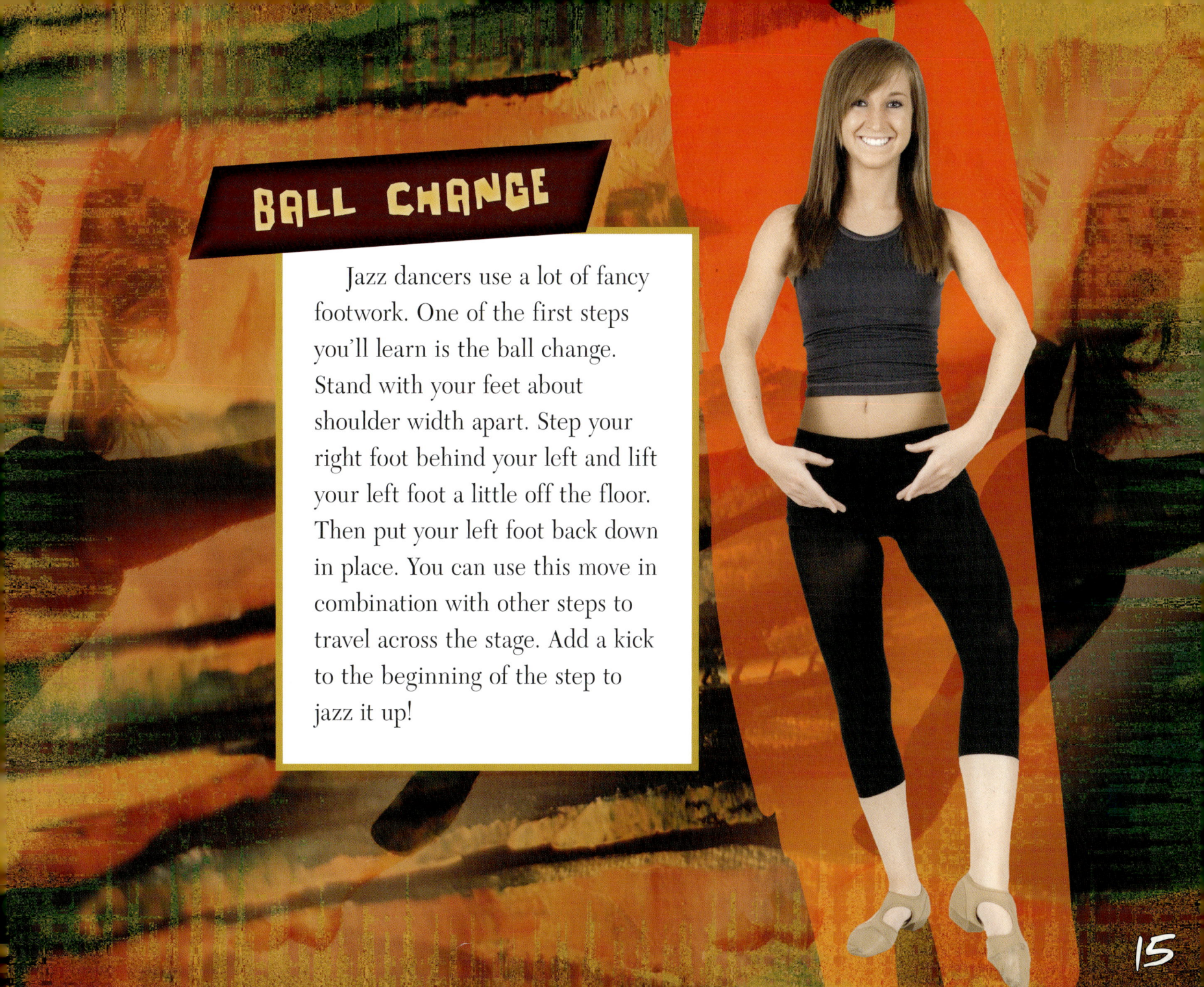

BALL CHANGE

Jazz dancers use a lot of fancy footwork. One of the first steps you'll learn is the ball change. Stand with your feet about shoulder width apart. Step your right foot behind your left and lift your left foot a little off the floor. Then put your left foot back down in place. You can use this move in combination with other steps to travel across the stage. Add a kick to the beginning of the step to jazz it up!

JAZZ SQUARE

Another footwork sequence is the jazz square. You will make a square pattern as you step. Start with your feet together. Step with your right foot across your left. Next, step your left foot back behind your right. Then pick up your right foot and cross it back diagonally. Finally, step your left foot in front of your right.

PAS DE BOURRÉE

Another traveling step is the pas de bourrée. The pas de bourrée is a series of three steps usually done with knees bent and heels lifted. First, step your left foot forward and across the right. Then step your right foot out to the side. Finally, step forward with your left foot. If you want to add arm movements, start with them straight out to the side. As your foot steps across, bend your arms into your chest at your elbows. When you step your other foot out, extend your arms back out to the side.

Chapter Four

Beyond Classic

Contemporary

Combined with other dance elements, jazz dance tells a story all its own. Contemporary and lyrical are softer sides of jazz. Many of the movements used in lyrical and contemporary are borrowed from ballet and modern dance. In contemporary, a dancer combines jazz isolations with modern motion and ballet technique. You'll often see a contemporary dancer walk with flexed feet or roll on the floor.

LYRICAL

With lyrical jazz, a dancer also combines ballet, modern, and jazz dance techniques.

These three techniques form a dance that is like physical poetry. Lyrical dancers perform slow, rounded movements. A lyrical routine will often focus on balance and control to make the dance a flowing performance.

JAZZ/FUNK

This funky style mixes hip-hop attitude with jazz technique. Jazz/funk steps are punchy and hard-hitting. This type of dance is usually performed to hip-hop or pop music. You can expect jazz/funk to be fast-paced. Usher, Janet Jackson, and Justin Timberlake all perform jazz/funk in their music videos.

THEATRICAL

Jazzin' up Broadway

Jazz dance is an important part of modern Broadway musicals. Plays like *Chicago* and *Hairspray* rely heavily on jazz dancing to tell part of the story. Some dance studios across the country actually teach classes they call Broadway jazz. These classes focus on routines that have been done in musicals. Dancers learn to develop performance techniques and facial expressions. It's kind of like a combination dance and acting class.

Theatrical jazz mixes up classic jazz with today's popular moves. Often, theatrical jazz dancers are trained in ballet so they can pull off difficult steps. And most musicals require dancers to sing in the chorus. If you want to dance on Broadway, you better warm up those vocal chords too!

BIGGER MOVES

TUCK

A more advanced jazz routine features jumps, kicks, and turns. One fun jump is a tuck. Start with both knees bent. Then jump into the air. As you jump, tuck your feet right up to your bottom. Then land back in the starting position.

GRAND BATTEMENT

One of the most popular kicks is the grand battement. If you are flexible and have stretched your legs, try this move. Stand with your feet together and arms out to your side. Brush your right foot against the floor as you kick it up toward your shoulder. Control your leg by keeping both knees straight and your stomach tight.

CHAINÉ

Chainé turns are linked together like a chain. To start, step to the right, turning your body half way around. Then step with your left foot to turn your body the rest of the way around. Finish the move by putting your left foot flat on the ground and gliding your right foot back to the front.

To keep from getting dizzy, try spotting. Focus on a spot ahead of you. As you turn, keep your eyes on the spot for as long as you can. At the last possible moment, whip your head around and refocus on the same spot.

Jazz Hands

You've probably heard the phrase "jazz hands" before. Using your hands is a big part of the attitude in jazz dancing. Jazz hands is a technique where you spread your fingers out wide and point your palms forward. There are variations of this move too. You can do jazz hands facing down or with the backside of your hand pointing forward. Each variation gives a move a unique look.

CHAPTER FIVE

Takin' It to the Next Step

Learning all the techniques for jazz dance takes many years. In fact, professionals train every day. They are always working to explore new ways to move their bodies. After high school, many dancers go on to study at colleges and universities.

But training doesn't stop there. After college, dancers often go to professional dance schools to learn from master jazz dance trainers. Students at these schools often tour with the school's dance company to show off what they have learned.

Famous Company

Giordano Jazz Dance Chicago is a well-known jazz dance company. Dancers from across the country come to study jazz dance from the legendary Gus Giordano. Since 1962, dancers from the company have toured the United States and many other countries around the world. Giordano's technique, which focuses on training the entire body, is taught in many dance studios across the country.

Jazz All Around

Love jazz dancing? There are plenty of places to check it out. Touring musicals will have plenty of jazz dancing. Performances are probably playing in a theater near you. Need a couple of suggestions? Check out *Hairspray* or *The Lion King*.

Also, professional jazz dance companies give performances in most major cities. Giordano Jazz Dance Chicago or Savage Jazz Dance Company from Oakland, California, are only two of many companies out there. Check out their Web sites to see if they're dancing in a city nearby.

But getting up and doing some moves of your own is the best way to enjoy jazz dance. You can take some classes at a local dance studio. Or check out your school's dance team. But remember, jazz dance is all about personal style. So wherever you dance, do what feels right for your body. Get out there and jazz it up!

Glossary

battement (bat-MAHN) — extending the leg

body isolation (BOD-ee eye-suh-LAY-shun) — a move that separates one part of your body from the rest

chainé (sheh-NAY) — a series of turns

pas de bourrée (PAH DUH boo-RAY) — a step that allows a dancer to move across the floor

syncopate (SING-kuh-pate) — to stress beats that are not normally stressed

Fast Facts

Jazz dance helped make Paula Abdul famous. Abdul is an accomplished jazz dancer. She has done choreography for music videos for a number of pop stars, as well as doing jazz dance in her own videos.

Many jazz dances in the 1960s, such as the Monkey and the Pony, imitated animals.

Read More

Andreu, Helene. *Jazz Dance Styles and Steps for Fun.* Bloomington, Ind.: 1st Books, 2002.

Cutcher, Jenai. *Gotta Dance!: The Rhythms of Jazz and Tap.* The Curtain Call Library of Dance. New York: Rosen, 2004.

Garofoli, Wendy. *Dance Team.* Dance. Mankato, Minn.: Capstone Press, 2008.

Internet Sites

FactHound offers a safe, fun way to find Internet sites related to this book. All of the sites on FactHound have been researched by our staff.

Here's how:

1. Visit *www.facthound.com*
2. Choose your grade level.
3. Type in this book ID **1429613521** for age-appropriate sites. You may also browse subjects by clicking on letters, or by clicking on pictures and words.
4. Click on the **Fetch It** button.

Facthound will fetch the best sites for you!

About the Author

Wendy Garofoli is a writer for *Dance Magazine*, *Dance Spirit*, *Cheer Biz News*, and *Dance Retailer News*. She was the captain of the national champion New York University Purple & White Dance Team and has studied jazz for nearly 20 years. She continues to teach and choreograph for various all-star and collegiate dance teams.

INDEX

Broadway musicals, 4, 21, 28

clothing, 10

Cole, Jack, 7, 8

dance companies, 4, 26, 27, 28

history, 4, 6

Lindy hop, 6

moves
　ball change, 15
　body isolations, 14, 18
　chainé turns, 24
　grand battement, 23
　jazz hands, 25
　jazz square, 16
　pas de bourrée, 17
　tuck, 22

music, 4, 6, 8, 14, 20

shoes, 10

styles of jazz dance
　classic, 8, 9, 10, 14
　contemporary, 8, 10, 18
　jazz/funk, 8, 10, 20
　lyrical, 10, 18, 19
　theatrical, 21, 28

warm-ups, 12–13

MAY 1 5 2009